# Blackberry Banquet

By Terry Pierce

Illustrated by Lisa Downey

In a wee green wood,
near a stream so blue,
grows a blackberry bush,
shining bright with dew.

On limbs so full,
hanging plump and sweet,
are the juiciest berries
any critter could eat.

Mouse appears and she reaches high.
That munching mouse gives a merry sigh.
*Squeak! Mmm-mm!*

Bluebird lights and he eats his fill.
That busy-busy bird sings a happy trill.
*Tweet! Mmm-mm!*
*Squeak! Mmm-mm!*

Squirrel skips into the brambles thick.
That snacking squirrel gives a great big lick.
*Slurp! Mmm-mm!*
*Tweet! Mmm-mm!*
*Squeak! Mmm-mm!*

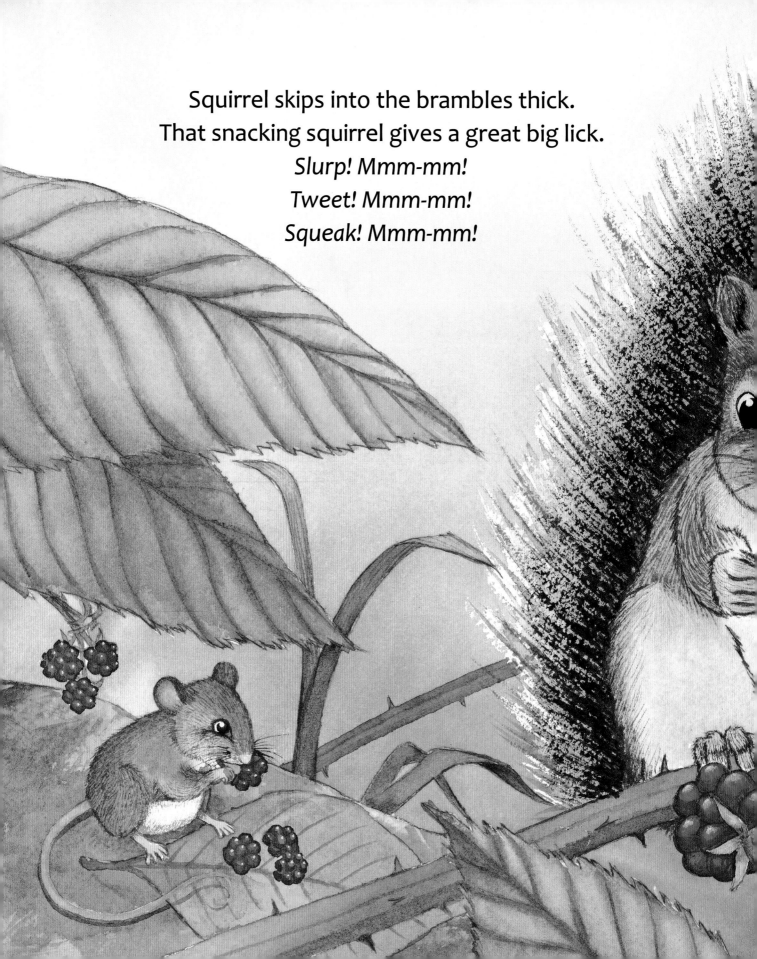

Fox trots in and takes a tasty nip.
That feasting fox makes a joyful yip.
*Yip! Mmm-mm!*
*Slurp! Mmm-mm!*
*Tweet! Mmm-mm!*
*Squeak! Mmm-mm!*

Deer strolls in with an appetite.
That dining deer takes a great big bite.
*Chomp! Mmm-mm!*
*Yip! Mmm-mm!*
*Slurp! Mmm-mm!*
*Tweet! Mmm-mm!*
*Squeak! Mmm-mm!*

Bear tramps up—

Bear? Where?

There!

Bear scares Deer!

Deer frightens Fox!

Fox shocks Squirrel!

Squirrel bumps Bird!

Bird muddles Mouse!

Mouse flings berries!

There's a blackberry bush,
in a wee green wood,
where the berries are gone
'cause they taste so good!

*Mmm-mmm-mm!*

# For Creative Minds

## Blackberries

We are not the only animals that enjoy eating blackberries! Some other familiar blackberry-eating animals include those mentioned in the book: robins, cardinals, skunks, red foxes, and raccoons.

The fruits grow as clusters of **drupelets** on prickly shrubs.

Unripe blackberries are actually red and can be easily confused with raspberries.

Blackberries turn a dark purple and have a white core that runs through the center when ripe.

Ripe berries may be picked during the summer or even in early fall in some areas.

Do not pick and eat berries unless an adult is positive that they are edible (some berries can be poisinous) and haven't been sprayed with pesticides.

Only pick enough berries that you are going to eat and always leave some berries to reseed the plant.

## How do we eat blackberries...

Just the berries—fresh picked!    Over ice cream    Cakes/muffins/pies

Jam    Blackberry syrup    Smoothies

## Blackberry Smoothie

Fresh berry smoothies are a great treat to beat the heat on a hot, summer day! They are even better with fresh picked berries.

1 c. vanilla yogurt, ice cream, or milk
1/2 c. fresh or frozen blackberries
1 small to medium banana
2 to 3 Tbs. sugar (to taste depending on berries)

Use a blender on puree or high speed to mix.

# Plants are the bottom of the food web

Are you surprised that a bear eats blackberries? Many people are! Whether an animal eats plants or animals, plants are the bottom of all food webs—no matter what habitat (yes, even in the ocean). Even some large animals like deer only eat plants.

Green plants are called **producers** because they make their own food (sugar) using sunlight, air, minerals, and water.

Animals cannot make their own food. They must eat plants or other animals for energy. They are called consumers. There are three kinds of consumers.

- Animals that only eat plants are called **herbivores** or **primary consumers**.
- Animals that eat other animals are called **carnivores**. Carnivores that eat herbivores are called secondary consumers.
- Carnivores that eat other carnivores are called tertiary consumers.

Animals that eat both plants and animals are called omnivores (omni means "both").

**Decomposers** such as mushrooms feed on dead plants and animals, turning them back into the soil to feed the plants. That starts the cycle all over again!

1. Which animal is a **herbivore:** black bear, deer, or fox? _____

2. A gray fox might eat which animals? _____

# Plants and Animals

Just like in the story, many animals eat plants or parts of plants. All the animals ate the fruit from the blackberry shrub.

Some animals make their homes in plants. *Can you think of some animals that live in plants (trees, bushes, grasses, etc.)?* Some animals might live in a burrow or a den but the opening is hidden by plants. Other animals might use pieces of plants to build their nests or homes.

Plants give us oxygen to breathe!

Humans eat plants, too! *Can you think of some foods that we eat that come from plants?* We eat seeds and fruit, just like the animals in the book. We also eat nuts, leaves (lettuce), flowers (broccoli), or stems (celery).

Animals often hide in plants for protection.

# How do animals help plants?

Plants need to spread their seeds far away from the parent plant so that the seeds have the room, sunlight, and energy to grow into new plants. Animals help do this by carrying seeds away from the plants.

Sometimes seeds stick to the fur or hair of an animal. The seeds later fall off and hopefully will grow.

When animals eat the fruit or seeds and then go to the bathroom, they leave the seeds far away from the parent plant.

Some animals may bury seeds to eat later but then forget about them. Then the seeds may grow.

# Are plants always good?

Some plants naturally occur in certain areas. We call them **native** plants. Sometimes plants grow in areas where they are not native and we call them **non-native** plants. Some non-natives, including several species of blackberry, are also invasive in that they take over an area. Not all non-natives are invasive. In some places, certain types of blackberries are considered to be invasive. If planting blackberry bushes, please always use plants that are native to the area you live.

Invasive plants can grow so much that they take the space, sunlight, and energy that native plants need to grow. This could threaten the native plants.

If native plants can't grow, the animals that depend on those plants for food and shelter could also become threatened.

Blackberry bushes can become very brambly and sometimes grow near water sources. In some places, this could make it difficult for animals to get to their food or water. This is another reason why invasive plants can sometimes become a problem.

To Greg, my berry-picking buddy; thanks for all the sweet memories—TP
For my mom and dad—LD

Thanks to Jamie Little, Interpretive Coordinator for Oregon Parks and Recreation; and to Alison Heimowitz, Education Coordinator at Clackamas Community College's John Inskeep Environmental Learning Center, and Treasurer of the Environmental Education Association of Oregon for verifying the accuracy of the information in this book.

Publisher's Cataloging-In-Publication Data

Pierce, Terry.
Blackberry banquet / by Terry Pierce ; illustrated by Lisa Downey.

p. : col. ill. ; cm.

Summary: Forest animals enjoy the sweet, plump fruit of a wild blackberry bush. But what happens when a bear arrives to take part in the feast? Includes "For Creative Minds" section with fun facts, a recipe and information on plants and animals.

Interest age level: 004-008.
Interest grade level: P-3.
ISBN: 978-1-934359-70-9 (hardcover)
ISBN: 978-1-934359-28-0 (pbk.)

1. Blackberries--Juvenile fiction. 2. Food chains (Ecology)--Juvenile fiction. 3. Forest animals-- Juvenile fiction. 4. Bears--Juvenile fiction. 5. Blackberries--Fiction. 6. Food chain (Ecology)--Fiction. 7. Forest animals--Fiction. 8. Bears--Fiction. 9. Stories in rhyme. I. Downey, Lisa. II. Title.

PZ7.P614642 Bl 2008
[E]            2008920383

Printed in China

Sylvan Dell Publishing
976 Houston Northcutt Blvd., Suite 3
Mt. Pleasant, SC 29464